Hands-On STEM

# FOCUS ON LIGHT

by Patricia Hutchison

FOCUS READERS

# FOCUS READERS

www.focusreaders.com



Focus Readers is distributed by North Star Editions:
sales@northstareditions.com | 888-417-0195

Produced for Focus Readers by Red Line Editorial.

Content Consultant: Bruce Bolon, Associate Professor of Physics, Hamline University

Photographs ©: EugenP/Shutterstock Images, cover, 1; Maxiphoto/iStockphoto, 4–5; Africa Studio/Shutterstock Images, 7, 29; MarioGuti/iStockphoto, 8–9; ttsz/iStockphoto, 11; PeterHermesFurian/iStockphoto, 13; aluxum/iStockphoto, 15; SerrNovik/iStockphoto, 17; ewg3D/iStockphoto, 19; Pat_Hastings/iStockphoto, 20; jophil/iStockphoto, 22–23; AtnoYdur/iStockphoto, 25; Red Line Editorial, 27

**ISBN**
978-1-63517-284-3 (hardcover)
978-1-63517-349-9 (paperback)
978-1-63517-479-3 (ebook pdf)
978-1-63517-414-4 (hosted ebook)

**Library of Congress Control Number: 2017935115**

Printed in the United States of America
Mankato, MN
June, 2017

## About the Author

Patricia Hutchison taught elementary science for more than 10 years. She continues to teach through the books she writes. She enjoys researching new subjects and writing about them in ways children can understand.

# TABLE OF CONTENTS

CHAPTER 1

# DARKNESS AND LIGHT

It is a stormy night. Rain pounds against the window. Thunder crashes overhead. Suddenly, a flash of lightning appears in the sky. The lamp goes out. All the colors in the room disappear.

Lightning can light up a dark sky.

Everything looks black. The electricity is off. But after a few minutes, the lamp flickers back on. The objects in the room are now visible. Everything is colorful again.

Light is the opposite of darkness. Light is what makes colors possible. Without light, our eyes would not work. That is why the room looked black when the lamp went out.

A living room would not be visible without light.

CHAPTER 2

# PARTICLES AND WAVES

All objects give off and take in **electromagnetic waves**. There are many types of these waves. But humans cannot see most of them. These waves include X-rays, radio waves, and many others.

**Scientists use large dishes to collect electromagnetic waves from far away.**

The waves humans can see are known as the visible **spectrum**. These waves also have a simpler name. They are called light.

Each color in the visible spectrum has a different **wavelength**. A wavelength is the length of one complete cycle of a wave. The colors in the visible spectrum have very short wavelengths. The wavelengths are **microscopic**. But other wavelengths can be much longer.

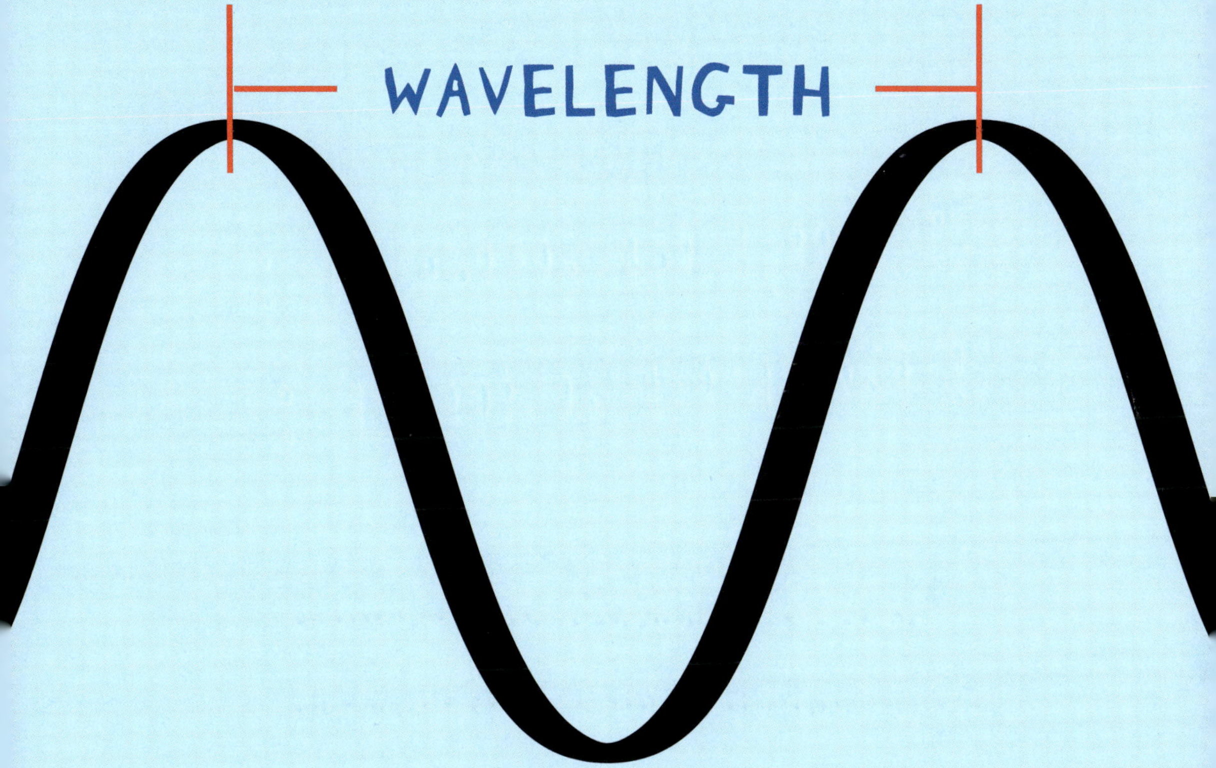


**Red light has a wavelength of approximately 700 nanometers. For comparison, a piece of paper is approximately 90,000 nanometers thick.**

For example, radio wavelengths can be hundreds of feet long.

Electromagnetic waves carry energy. The waves are sometimes called rays or beams. They are made up of tiny particles called **photons**.

All colors travel at approximately the same speed in air. But they travel slower in water or glass. Red light has the longest wavelength of the colors in the rainbow. Violet light has the shortest wavelength. Red light moves more

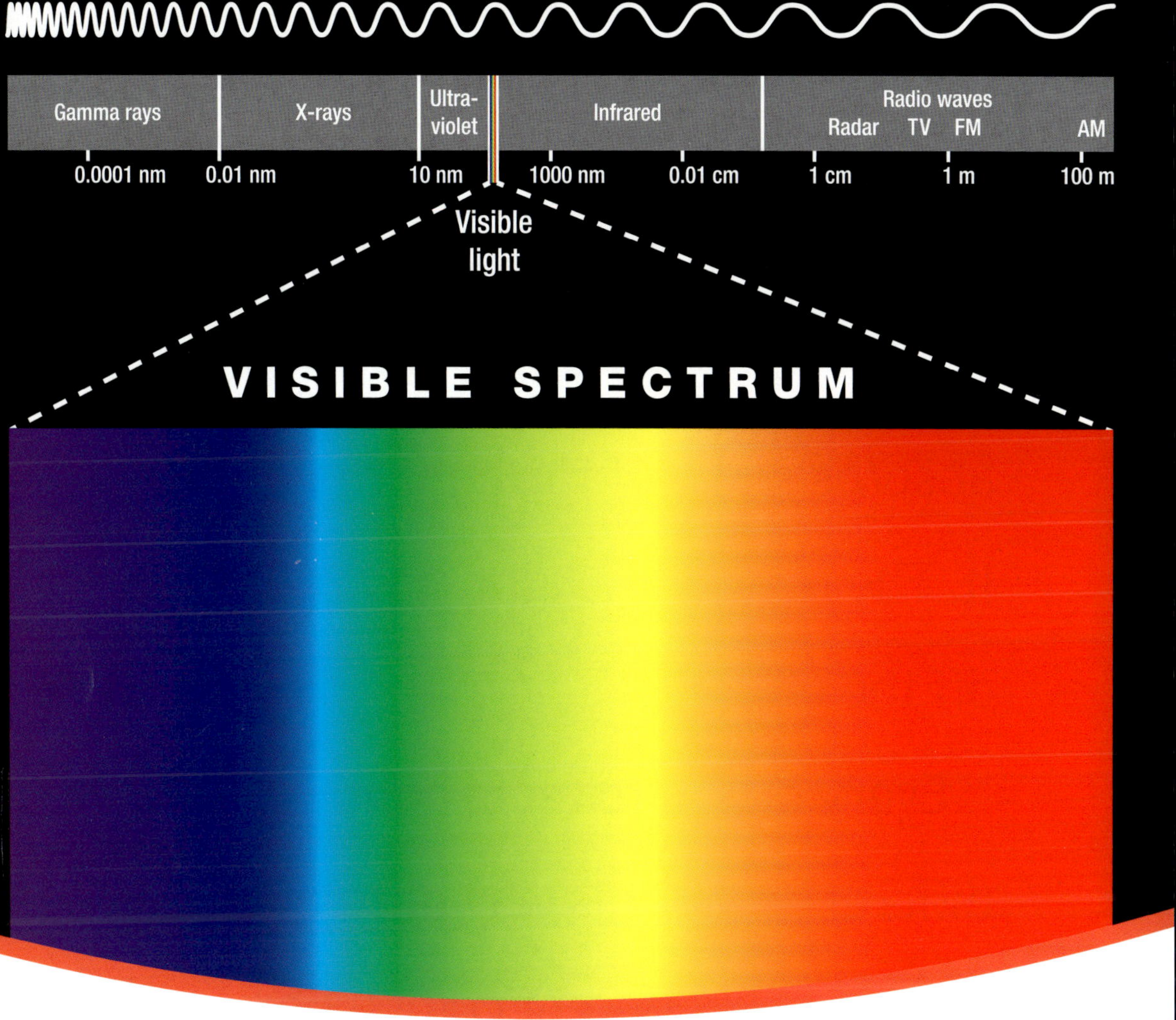


**Humans can see only a small part of the electromagnetic spectrum.**

quickly through water than violet light does.

Light rays usually move in a straight line. These rays hit objects in their path. An object usually absorbs some of the light that hits it. The rest of the light may **reflect** off the object.

Every object reflects light differently. That is why different objects are different colors. For example, a pumpkin reflects more orange light. A banana reflects more yellow light.

These apples absorb most light but reflect red light.

A black object absorbs most of the light that hits it. But a white object does the opposite. It reflects most of the light that hits it.

A shiny surface also reflects most light. A mirror is one example. But a mirror appears different than a white object. That is because a mirror's surface is very smooth.

Many objects do not allow light to pass through them. That is why they cast shadows. But light can pass through some objects.

A mirror reflects most of the light that hits its surface.

For example, light can pass through a thin sheet of paper. Light can also pass through glass and some types of plastic.

Objects may give off light when they are very hot. The sun is one example. It is a star. It gives off light and other electromagnetic waves. These waves have energy. The energy makes life on Earth possible.

Light rays can also bend, or **refract**. This happens when

A heated horseshoe gives off light.

light moves through one transparent substance to another.

These straws appear to be bent because light rays are being refracted.

For example, air and water are two see-through substances. Suppose light rays move from the air into water. The light rays will slow down and change direction. That's why a straw looks broken when it's in a glass of water.

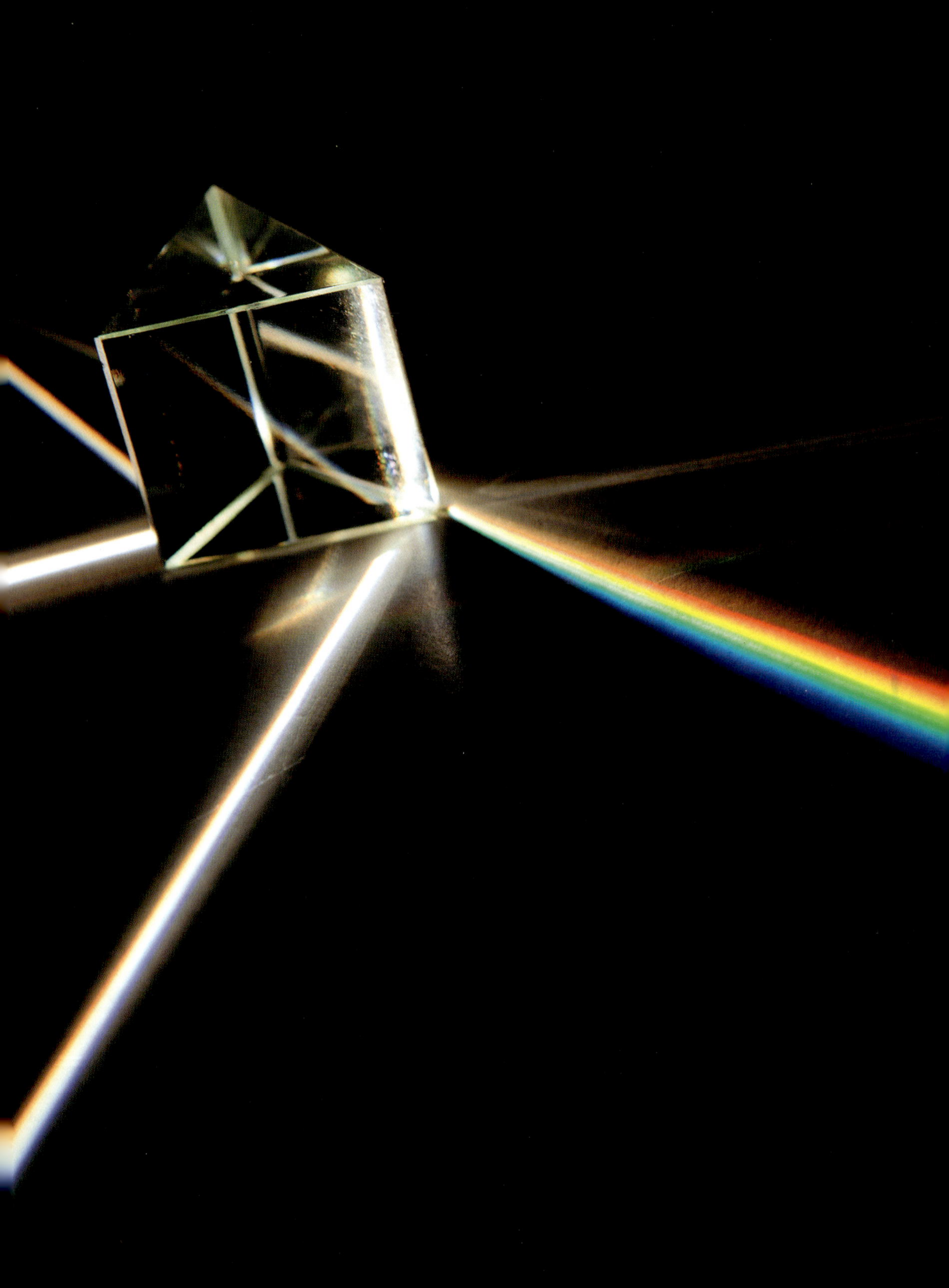

CHAPTER 3

# RAINBOWS AND X-RAYS

A rainbow shows the colors of the visible spectrum. The light from the sun moves through the air. Then it moves through millions of raindrops. The light is refracted. It is separated into seven colors.

**When white light shines into a prism, the light is separated into all colors of the rainbow.**

They are red, orange, yellow, green, blue, indigo, and violet. When your back is to the sun, your eyes see the colorful rainbow across the sky.

X-rays are part of the electromagnetic spectrum humans can't see. Doctors find X-rays useful. They use a machine to pass an X-ray beam through the body. The rays travel easily through skin and muscle. But bones absorb X-rays. They cast a white shadow on the film used to capture them.

Doctors have been using X-rays since the 1890s.

Doctors can see a picture of the bone to tell if it is broken.

SCIENCE IN ACTION!

# MAKING A COLOR WHEEL

What would you see if you mixed the colors of the rainbow together? Do this experiment to find out. Be sure to get help from an adult.

**Step 1:** Draw a circle on a piece of poster board. Carefully cut out the circle.

**Step 2:** Use a pencil to lightly divide the circle into six equal parts, similar to a pie.

**Step 3:** Color each space in this order: yellow, orange, red, purple, blue, and green.

**Step 4:** Push a thumbtack through the center of your color wheel. Pin the wheel to the top of a pencil's eraser.

A color wheel appears to be white when it spins quickly.

**Step 5:** Put the pencil between your palms. Slide your palms back and forth. Spin the pencil as fast as you can. Watch what happens to the color wheel.

What color did you see? Is this the color you thought you would see? How can you explain what happened? What do you think would happen if you put the colors in a different order on your color wheel?

## FOCUS ON

# LIGHT

*Write your answers on a separate piece of paper.*

1. Write a postcard to a friend describing the main ideas of Chapter 2.
2. Would you want to be able to see X-rays? Why or why not?
3. What happens when light rays hit a shiny object?
   - **A.** Most of the light rays bend.
   - **B.** Most of the light rays reflect.
   - **C.** Most of the light rays are absorbed.
4. Why can't you see a rainbow if the sun is directly overhead?
   - **A.** because the sun can't shine down through the raindrops
   - **B.** because raindrops will reflect the light instead of refracting it
   - **C.** because you can't turn your back to the sun when it is overhead

5. What does **visible** mean in this book?

*But after a few minutes, the lamp flickers back on. The objects in the room are now **visible**.*

A. able to be seen
B. dark
C. absorbed

6. What does **transparent** mean in this book?

*This happens when light moves through one **transparent** substance to another. For example, air and water are two see-through substances.*

A. hazy
B. clear
C. refracted

*Answer key on page 32.*

# GLOSSARY

**electromagnetic waves**
Waves that have both electric and magnetic properties.

**microscopic**
Too small to see without a microscope.

**photons**
Particles that make up light rays.

**reflect**
To bounce off of something.

**refract**
To change the direction of a wave when it passes from one material into another.

**spectrum**
A range that changes gradually from one end to the other.

**wavelength**
The length of one cycle, or one complete repetition, of a wave.

# TO LEARN MORE

## BOOKS

Koontz, Robin Michal. *Light in the Real World.* Minneapolis: Abdo Publishing, 2013.

Oxlade, Chris. *Experiments with Sound and Light.* New York: PowerKids Press, 2015.

Walker, Sally M. *Investigating Light.* Minneapolis: Lerner Publications, 2012.

## NOTE TO EDUCATORS

Visit **www.focusreaders.com** to find lesson plans, activities, links, and other resources related to this title.

# INDEX



**Answer Key: 1.** Answers will vary; **2.** Answers will vary; **3.** B; **4.** C; **5.** A; **6.** B